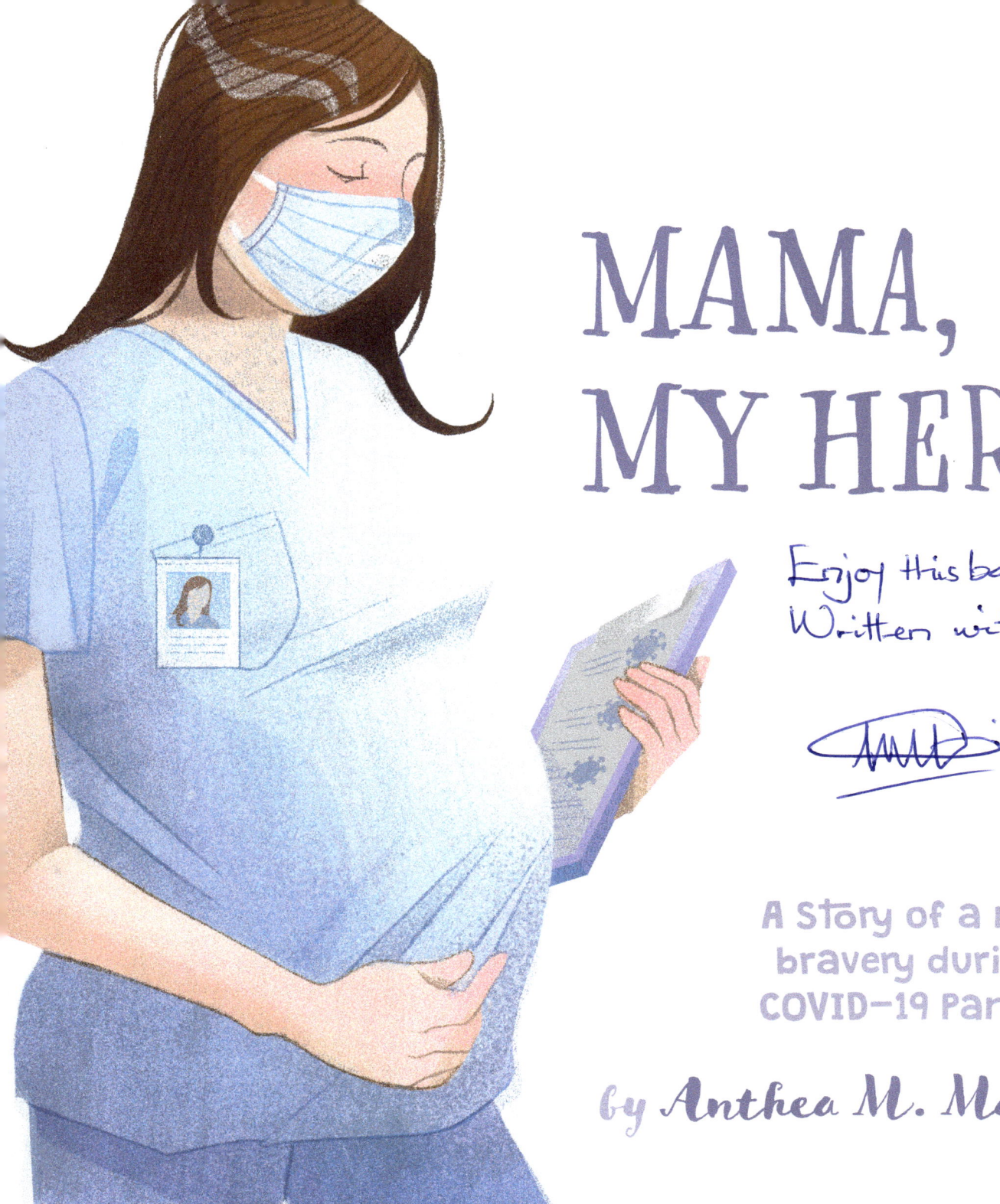

MAMA, MY HERO

Enjoy this book.
Written with love.

A story of a nurse's
bravery during the
COVID-19 Pandemic

by *Anthea M. Maseka*

DEDICATION

To my daughter-in-law, Julie, who, while pregnant,
worked tirelessly in an Albertan ICU ward
during the COVID-19 pandemic.

To Luwi, my first grandson.

And to all medical personnel and essential workers
risking their lives to save and serve others.

Mama is a nurse.
Helping sick people is what she does.
She carries me everywhere she goes.

I am little.
I am warm and safe.
I am snuggled in my mama's tummy.

But I am getting bigger every day.
And Mama is getting tired.

People everywhere are getting sick.
They are coughing and getting fevers.
The hospital is getting full.

"We must stay strong.
We must stay healthy.
Sick people need our help,"
Mama tells another nurse one morning.

"Time to work!" Mama says.

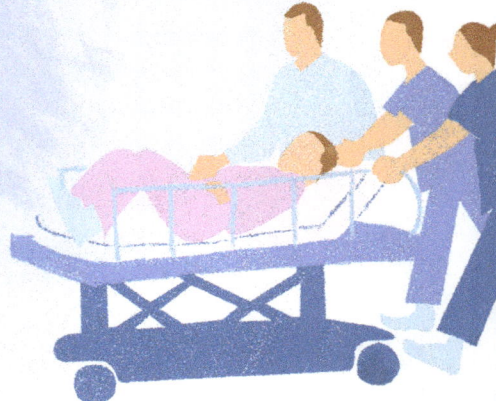

Mama puts on a mask to cover her mouth and nose.
She puts on gloves to protect her hands.
She puts on an apron over her scrubs.

Mama goes to comfort a man
who is not breathing well.
"It must be hard to breathe,"
she softly says.
"We will do our best to help
you get better again."

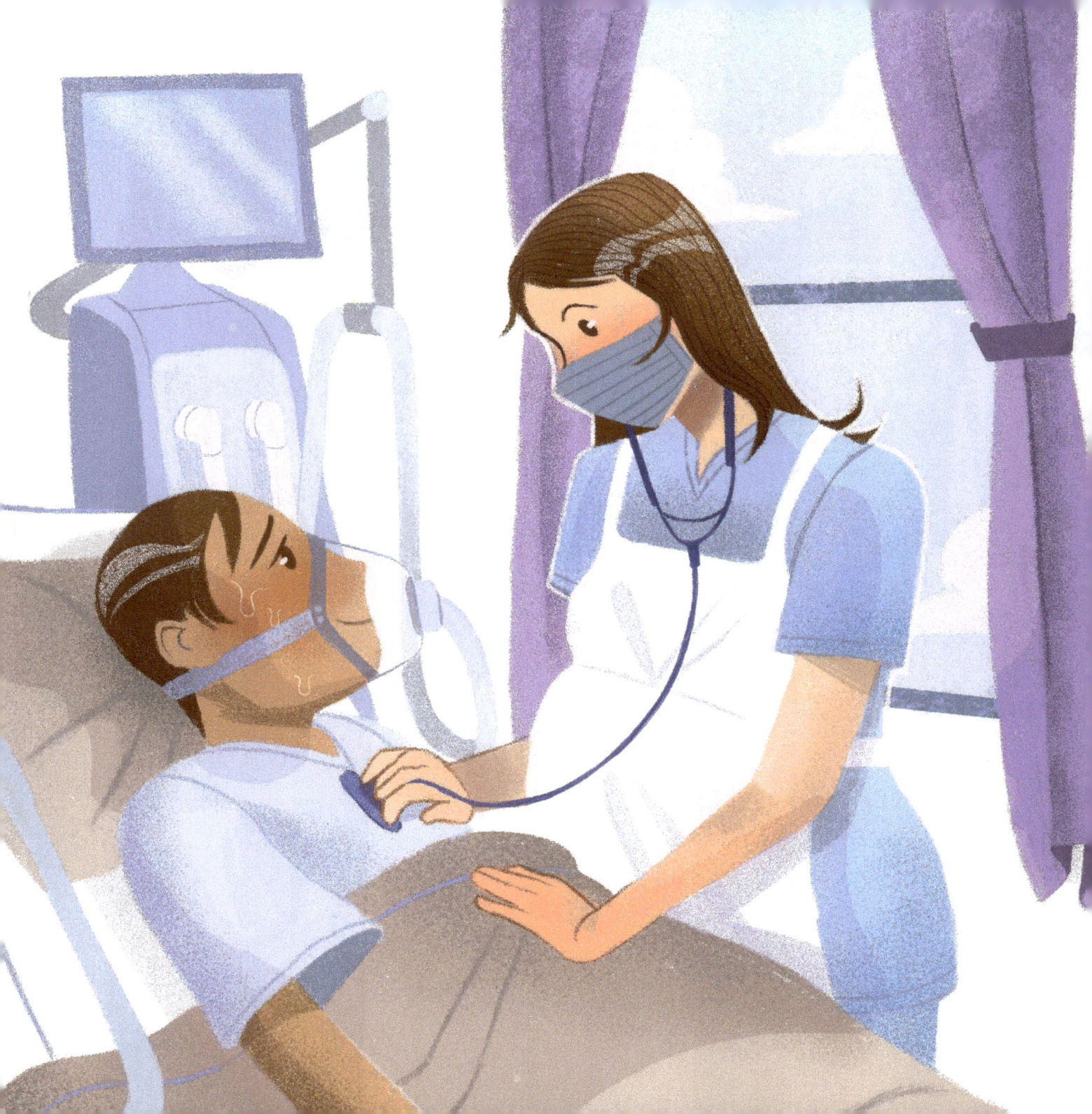

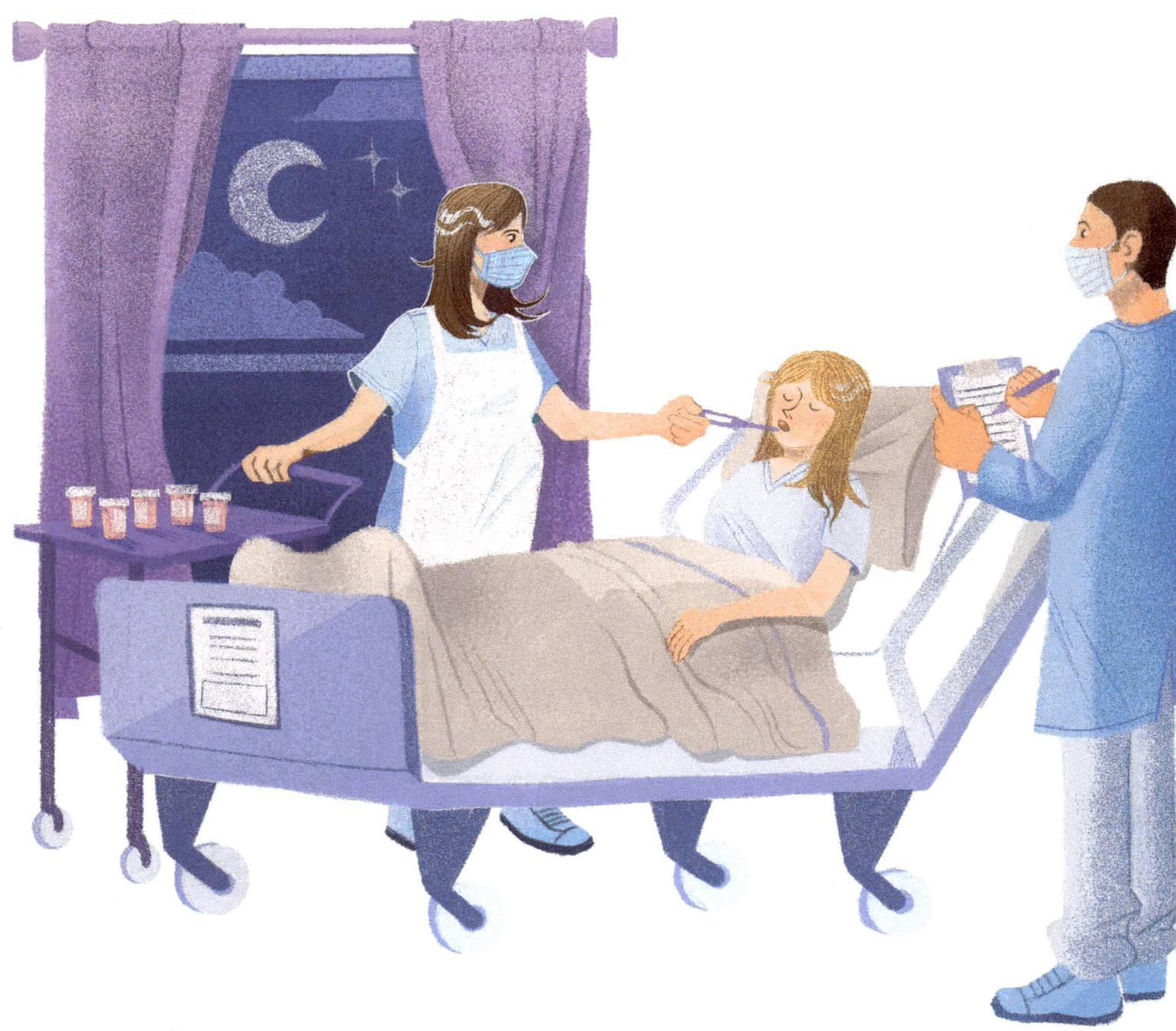

Work for Mama is very busy now.
A call comes from the next room.
Mama hurries to help.

I hear her kind voice say,
"I'm sorry you are still feeling this way.
It is time for your night medicine.
Very soon you will be feeling better."
Mama gives the medicine
to the sad, sick woman.

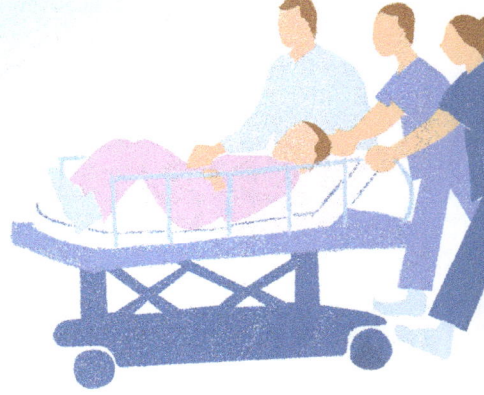

She tucks in her blanket
to keep the cold away.
"Good night," she smiles.
"I will be back tomorrow."

Mama leaves the room.
Her work for the day is done.

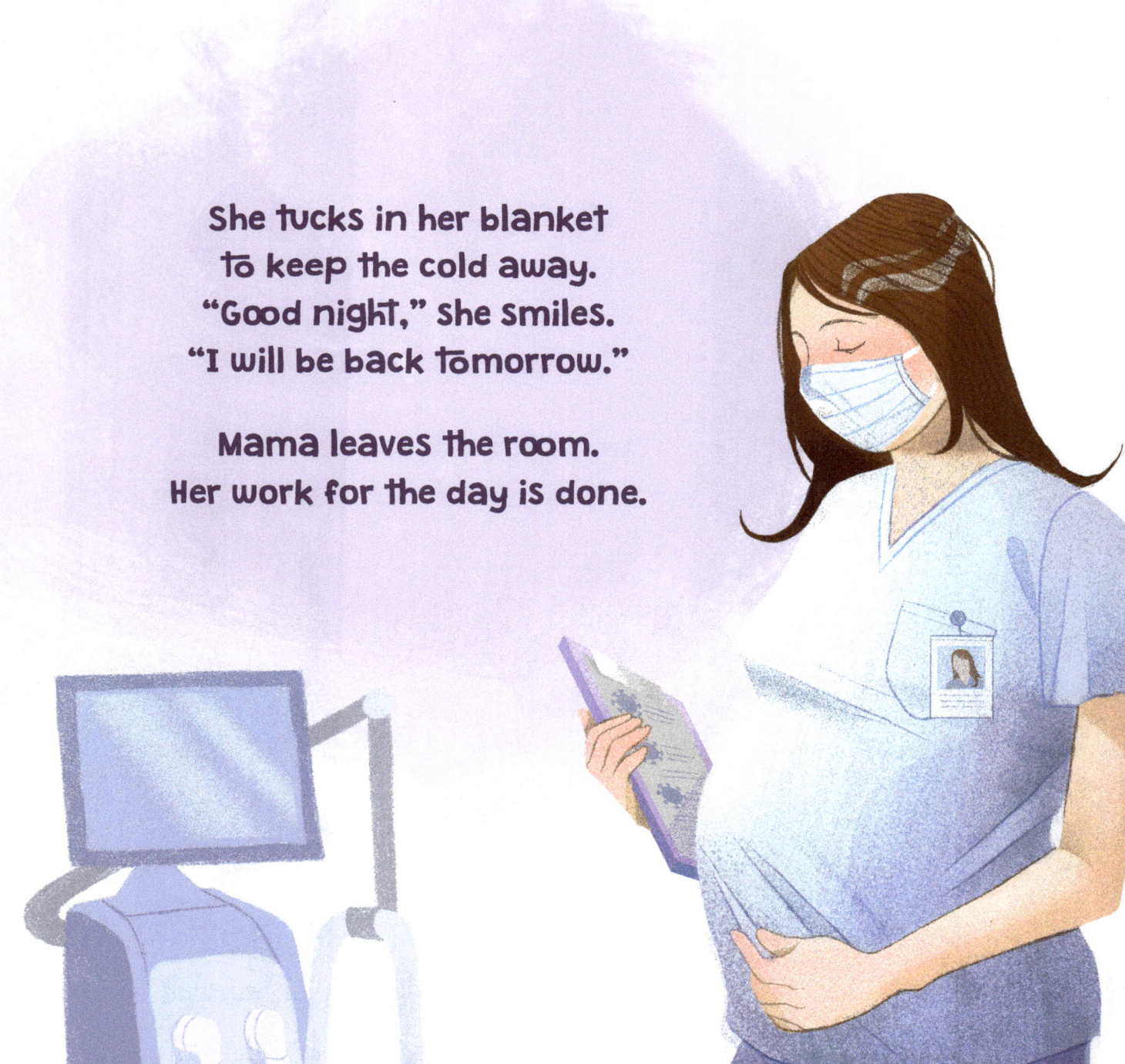

She takes off her gloves and washes her hands.

Mama then takes her mask from her face.

She removes the blue apron that covers her scrubs.
She drops it onto a pile.
It's a mountain of blue!

"Time to go and see Daddy,
little one," she says,
as she gently rubs her tummy.
I smile as she walks to the car.
Mama loves me, this I know.

Back at home,
Mama takes a bath.

She dresses in comfortable clothes
and goes to the kitchen.

Dada is happy to see Mama.
He puts a hot meal on the table.
"I have cooked your favourite food," Dada smiles.
Mama is happy. She sits at the table.

I listen as Mama talks to Dada.
She tells him stories of her day.
"It was busy," she says. "But I made it okay."

"I am proud of you," Dada says.
"I know you are kind.
I know you are brave."

Now Mama must rest from all the day's work.
She goes to bed, and soon she is asleep.
I love it as I snuggle in her tummy.
I am warm; I am safe.

Tomorrow is a new day.
A day in which Mama will help again.

My Mama. My hero!

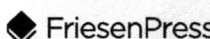 FriesenPress

Suite 300 - 990 Fort St
Victoria, BC, V8V 3K2
Canada

www.friesenpress.com

ISBN
978-1-5255-9674-2 (Hardcover)
978-1-5255-9673-5 (Paperback)
978-1-5255-9675-9 (eBook)

1. Fiction, Medical

Distributed to the trade by The Ingram Book Company

CPSIA information can be obtained
at www.ICGtesting.com
Printed in the USA
BVHW020350300621
610735BV00001B/2